80
70
60

Children are in a hurry to grow up.
Some children grow up and they seem happy,
they think:
'It's so good to be grown-up, to be free.
To decide everything for yourself!'
Other children, once they are grown-ups,
think exactly the opposite:
'It's so hard to be grown-up, to be free.
To decide everything for yourself!'

What is a Child?

Beatrice Alemagna

Tate Publishing

A child is a small person.
They are only small for a little while,
then they grow up.
They grow without even thinking about it.
Slowly and silently, their body grows taller.
A child is not a child forever.
One day, they change.

A child has small hands, small feet and small ears, but that does not mean they have small ideas.
Children's ideas can sometimes be very big.
They amuse the grown-ups and leave them open-mouthed, saying: 'Oh!'

Children want strange things:
to have shiny shoes, to eat lollipops for breakfast,
to hear the same story every evening.

Grown-ups, too, have strange ideas:
they take a bath every day,
they cook beans in butter,
they go to sleep without their yellow dog.
'But how is that possible?' children ask.

Children cry because a stone
has slipped into the water,
because shampoo stings their eyes,
because they are tired, because it is dark.
They cry loudly to make sure they are heard.
You need kind eyes to console them.
And a little night light by the bed.

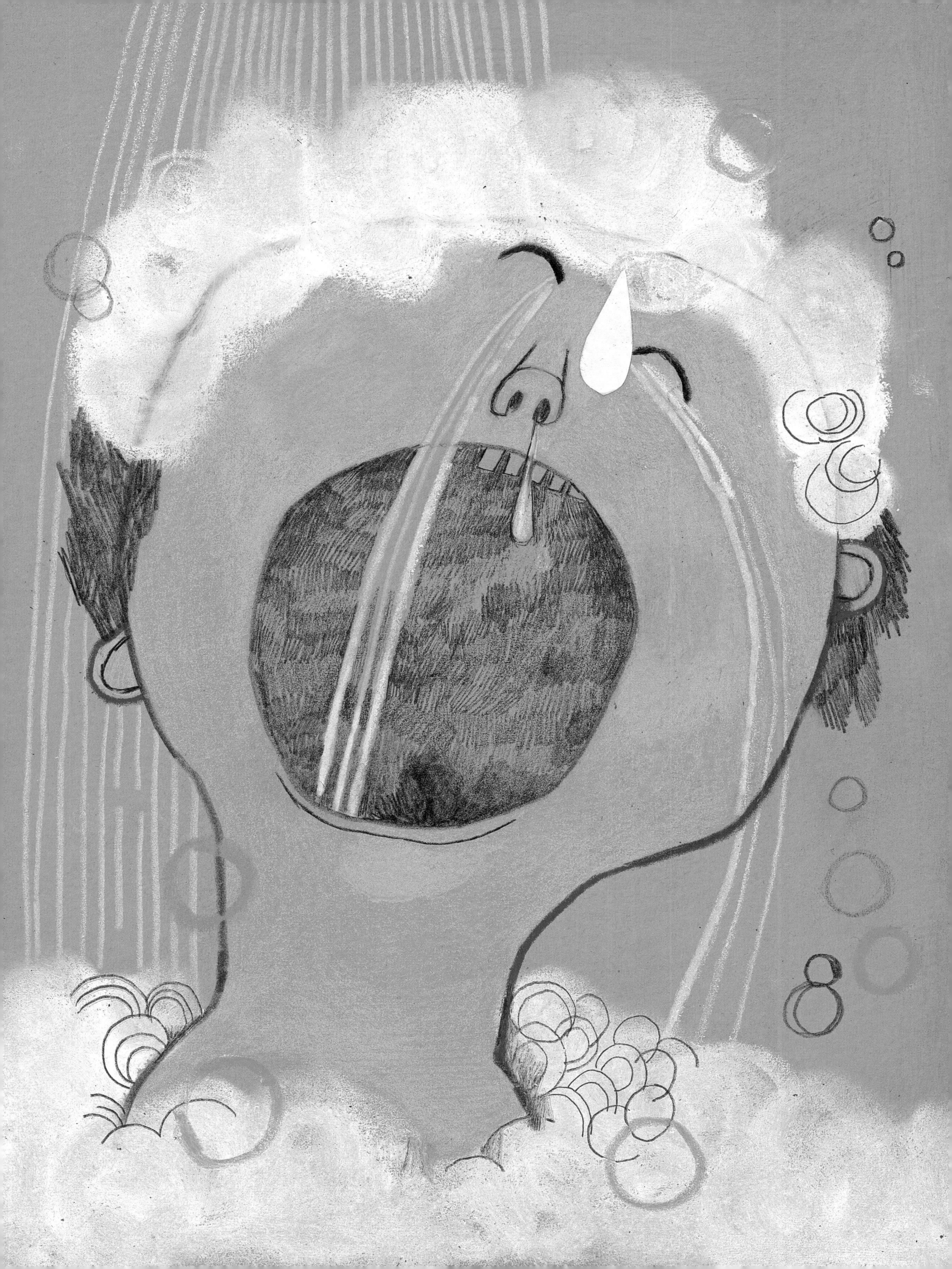

Grown-ups, on the other hand, like to sleep in the dark.
They hardly ever cry, not even when shampoo gets up their nose, and if this does happen they cry quietly.
So quietly that children don't notice.
Or they pretend they don't see anything.

Children are like sponges.
They soak everything in: bad moods, bad ideas,
other people's fears.
They seem to forget, but then everything
comes out again in their school bag,
or under the covers, or in front of a book.
Children want to be listened to with eyes wide open.

8+4 = 13

Children have little things, just like them:
a little bed, bright little books, a little umbrella,
a little chair.
Yet they live in a very big world: so big
that cities don't exist, buses go up into space
and stairs never end.

Children don't always like going to school.
Often children prefer to close their eyes
and sniff the grass, to shout and chase pigeons,
to listen to the faraway voice of shells,
to wrinkle up their noses in front of the mirror.

Children come in all shapes and sizes.
The children who decide not to grow up
will never grow up.
They keep a mystery inside them.
So that even as grown-ups they will be
moved by little things: a ray of sunshine
or a snowflake.

There are small, round, quiet children,
as well as tall and loud ones.
Children with glasses, freckles and braces on their
teeth that sparkle in the sunlight.

All children get frustrated
and angry sometimes.
Some children never want to go to bed.
There are others who never listen,
and children who sometimes break plates,
bowls and everything else.

All children are small people who will change some day.

They won't go to school any more,
but to work.
Hopefully they'll be happy, maybe they'll have
a beard or a bald head, or dyed green hair.
Maybe they'll make a fuss about odd things,
like a phone that doesn't ring. Or the traffic.

But why think about that now?

A child is a little person.
Right now, to fall asleep, they need kind eyes.
And a little night light by the bed.